Like **Butter** on **Pancakes**

by **Jonathan London**

illustrated by **G. Brian Karas**

PUFFIN BOOKS

PUFFIN BOOKS
Published by the Penguin Group
Penguin Putnam Inc., 375 Hudson Street, New York, New York 10014, U.S.A.
Penguin Books Ltd, 27 Wrights Lane, London W8 5TZ, England
Penguin Books Australia Ltd, Ringwood, Victoria, Australia
Penguin Books Canada Ltd, 10 Alcorn Avenue, Toronto, Ontario, Canada M4V 3B2
Penguin Books (N.Z.) Ltd, 182-190 Wairau Road, Auckland 10, New Zealand

Penguin Books Ltd, Registered Offices: Harmondsworth, Middlesex, England

First published in the United States of America by Viking,
a division of Penguin Books USA Inc., 1995
Published in Puffin Books, 1998

1 3 5 7 9 10 8 6 4 2

Text copyright © Jonathan London, 1995
Illustrations copyright © G. Brian Karas, 1995
All rights reserved

THE LIBRARY OF CONGRESS HAS CATALOGED THE VIKING EDITION AS FOLLOWS:
London, Jonathan.
Like butter on pancakes / by Jonathan London;
illustrated by G. Brian Karas.   p.   cm.
Summary: As the sun rises and sets, its rays highlight simple aspects and situations of
farm life, including the shadow of a cloud, the sizzle of bacon, and the dancing of spoons.
ISBN 0-670-85130-2
[1. Sun—Fiction. 2. Day—Fiction. 3. Farm life—Fiction.] I. Karas, G. Brian, ill. II. Title.
PZ7.L8423Lg 1995 [E]—dc20 94-9154 CIP AC

Puffin Books ISBN 0-14-055261-8

Printed in the United States of America

For Michael Patrick, with a smile and a nod to Pablo Neruda — J. L.

For Cecilia Yung, from Potatoes to Pancakes — G. B. K.

Beyond the rim
of morning
the sun ticks
the birds talk

and the spoons sleep nestled
in the kitchen drawers.

First light melts
like butter on pancakes,
spreads warm and yellow
across your pillow.

A woodpecker pecks
on a lone pine.
The sun ticks
the birds talk.

The rooster *ka-ka-kadoos*
on the henhouse roof.
A cloud drifts by
dragging a shadow.

**The sun ticks
the birds talk.
The cat purrs
rolling in the light.**

**Papa's kettle whistles
Mama's bacon sizzles
slippers whisper
across the kitchen floor.**

Rise 'n' shine!
Up 'n' at 'em!
Come 'n' get it!
Breakfast time!

You roll out of bed.
The smell of bacon
fills your sleepy head.
The sun ticks
the birds talk.

You pitter-patter
in your bunny slippers,
do the pajama dance
in a puddle of sun.

**The spoons dance with you
the knives and forks
the cups and saucers
and all the pretty dishes.**

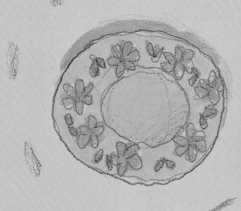

Then you sit down to eat,
swing your feet,
pour on the syrup
and dig right in.

When you lick your milk mustache you say, "All done!"

**The day has begun
and till the day is done
the sun ticks
the birds talk**

and you run and jump
and tumble in the hay.

The barnyard animals
hee-haw and neigh.
They honk and they cluck
and the cow jumps over

. . . your old red truck.

A bell rings. *Ting-a-ling!*
Time to wash up!
Supper time!
Come 'n' get it!

After supper
the night creeps in
and the moon spills milk
for the cat to drink.
Mama sings
in your soft, dark room.

**Papa hums
and you drift toward dreams
on your feather pillow.**

Beyond the rim
of evening
the sun sleeps
the birds too

and the spoons sleep nestled in the kitchen drawers.